1/22

When the Schools SHUT DOWN

A YOUNG GIRL'S STORY OF VIRGINIA'S "LOST GENERATION" AND THE *BROWN V. BOARD OF EDUCATION OF TOPEKA* DECISION

Written by **Yolanda Gladden**, as told to **Dr. Tamara Pizzoli**

Illustrated by **Keisha Morris**

HARPER

An Imprint of HarperCollinsPublishers

To Carrie Jefferson; Dorothy Alice Jefferson; my children, Kimiko,
Kaleb, and Jamal; my grandchildren; and the future generations to come.
A warm thank-you to Luana Horry.
—Yolanda

For Ms. Yolanda.
What a gift it was to collaborate on this book with you. Here's to the
truth and power of your stories—this one, and all the others you hold
that I hope you'll one day share with the world.
—Dr. Pizzoli

For my loving and supportive mom
—Keisha

When the Schools Shutdown: A Young Girl's Story of Virginia's "Lost Generation" and the *Brown v. Board of*
Education of Topeka Decision
Text copyright © 2022 by Dr. Tamara Pizzoli and Yolanda Gladden
Illustrations copyright © 2022 by Keisha Morris
Photographs: pages 36–37, courtesy of Yolanda Gladden; page 40, courtesy of *Richmond Times-Dispatch*
All rights reserved. Manufactured in Italy.
No part of this book may be used or reproduced in any manner whatsoever without written permission except
in the case of brief quotations embodied in critical articles and reviews. For information address HarperCollins
Children's Books, a division of HarperCollins Publishers, 195 Broadway, New York, NY 10007.
www.harpercollinschildrens.com
Library of Congress Control Number: 2020952905
ISBN: 978-0-06-301116-8
The artist used collaged tissue paper and Photoshop to create the digital illustrations for this book.
Typography by Rachel Zegar
21 22 23 24 25   RTLO   10 9 8 7 6 5 4 3 2 1
❖
First Edition

A child who only learns at school
is an uneducated child.
—West African proverb

The year Yolanda Gladden was born, the United States looked much different than it does today. The country's cars, clothes, land, and even laws reflected old ideas—some were classic, and others were simply cold.

WHITES ONLY

Yet, in that same year, on May 5, 1954, the US Supreme Court unanimously decided that separating children in public schools based on the color of their skin was no longer legally allowed. They called it the *Brown v. Board of Education of Topeka* decision. The world *seemed* to be changing.

And in Farmville, Virginia, Carrie Jefferson's world was growing.
Yolanda was the first of mama Carrie's three children. She was born with
beautiful brown skin and a crown of coily deep brown hair.

After Yolanda came her sister, Heldort, followed by a baby brother, Alexander. Growing up, Yolanda and her siblings knew not to mix too much in grown folks' business.

They had their own business to mind, like collecting firewood,

setting the table for dinner,

and making up fun games to play between chores.

But every now and then, Yolanda would catch bits and pieces of her mama's conversations with her aunt Dorothy and uncle Tank.

They'd talk about everything under the sun: recipes, religion, right and wrong. There was talk of love and of new laws.

In fact, Yolanda picked up a lot from paying attention to her family, her friends, and people in her neighborhood.

She learned how to swap five cents for a Mary Jane from Uncle Tank's convenience store. Yolanda would slurp down her favorite fizzy drink with such speed and satisfaction that Uncle Tank nicknamed her "Soda."

She learned that a new hairdo could make anyone look and feel like a queen at Aunt Magnolia's beauty salon.

And every day at home, Yolanda learned from watching her mother sew the entire family's clothes by hand that it didn't take a lot of money to look and feel like a million dollars.

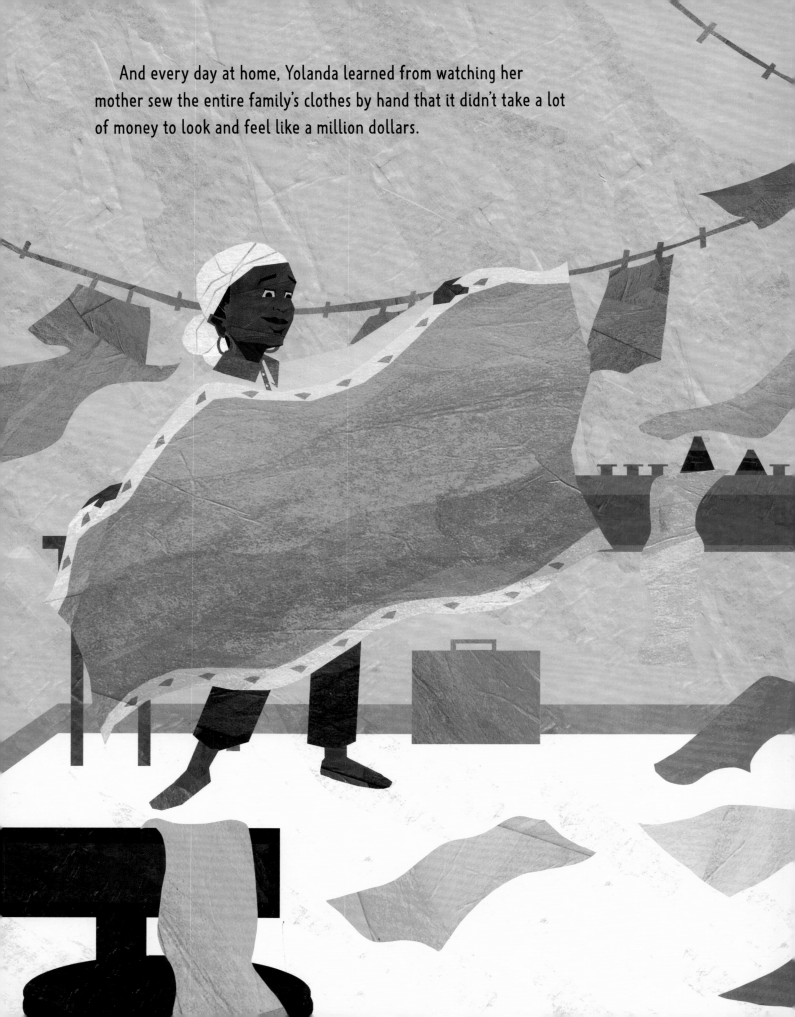

Watching her family members
taught Yolanda how to carry herself—
head high,
shoulders back,
spine straight.
Proud.

YOU
COUNT

The most important lessons came on Sunday mornings at First Baptist Church. Yolanda heard Bible stories of conflict and struggle, trouble and triumph. These same stories demonstrated power, resilience, faith, and love.

She would sit, wedged between her mother and siblings, listening to the tales of David and Goliath, Moses, Jonah, and Jesus Christ. If Yolanda or her siblings fidgeted or whispered, their mama would shoot a glare in their direction that needed no words at all.

As she grew, Yolanda noticed the world around her was divided into two distinct colors: black and white.

She knew from overhearing her mama, Uncle Tank, and Aunt Dorothy that sorting people based on color was nothing new in Farmville and that how each of the two groups lived and learned was quite different indeed.

When her mama was in school, the classrooms were cold enough to make one's teeth chatter; books were used, tattered, and torn; and school buses ran late or not at all.

1951, FARMVILLE, PRINCE EDWARD COUNTY

Mama and Aunt Dorothy, along with several other high school students, had decided to boycott. They refused to attend classes until their voices were heard and their learning materials improved.

Some people saw boycotts as nothing more than making mischief, but the students knew boycotting was necessary to make change.

Change can be speedy, or steady, or incredibly slow.
When Yolanda's mama and Aunt Dorothy graduated from high school
in 1953, the conditions of public schools in Prince Edward County were
still separate, still unequal, and still unfair.

1959, VIRGINIA

Yolanda didn't fully understand all the conversations she overheard, but in 1959—four years after the *Brown v. Board of Education* decision was made—she knew it was finally her turn to start school.

The new integration law was supposed to be a step in the right direction. But by the time the first official day of classes rolled around, everything had changed *again* in Prince Edward County.

White lawmakers demanded to keep children in Yolanda's town sorted by color. And to make sure they got their way, they **shut down** each of the public schools in Prince Edward County one by one.

How could Yolanda go to school when there was no school to go to?

It was then that Yolanda learned that because a law is legal doesn't mean it is just. And just because a law exists doesn't mean everyone will follow it.

In reaction to the school closings, some people hit the pavement to protest.

LINE UP FOR EDUCATION

WHY FIVE?

Others hit the books.

Black parents, teachers, and community members across the county rallied together and created their own education system—they started schools and learning centers just for them.

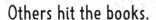

Sunday School
9:30 - 10:30

Black children of all ages met in church basements and even at one another's homes to attend school. From early morning to midafternoon, classes were in session.

Education was their right, and absolutely no one could keep them from

learning,

knowing,

and growing.

Yolanda wore the outfits her mother had sewn for her and showed up daily to her new school at First Baptist Church.

She was one of about twenty students from ages five to eleven. The students worked with the few materials they had—some borrowed and others barely functional. Yolanda and her classmates studied the three R's: reading, 'riting (writing), and 'rithmetic (arithmetic).

Her teacher Mrs. Herndon would say, "If you know your history, then you'll know where you're going."

Mrs. Womack, another teacher, taught her that the history of Black people did not begin or end with Africans being enslaved in America, and included a rich, vast, glorious past, present, and future.

KING

QUEEN

AARON DOUGLAS

JANE C. WRIGHT

AUGUSTA SAVAGE

VIVIEN THOMAS

Yolanda was intrigued by how many amazing and useful creations were invented by Black scholars, scientists, researchers, artists, and innovators. Like Marcus Garvey, she knew Black was a wonderful thing to be.

The schools in Prince Edward County were completely closed for five full years, but each school day, classes were under way at the community-created Black schools.

A breakthrough finally came in 1964, the same year Yolanda turned ten years old.

The Supreme Court ruled the school shutdown unconstitutional and demanded that all schools be reopened to all students.

In the new classes at the Prince Edward school, Black and white students were able to learn the same material in the same classrooms at the same time. Yolanda, who had been educated by her family, her church, and her community, passed each school exam with flying colors and was among the highest-achieving students in her class.

With the knowledge that opportunities to grow are all around and school can take place anywhere, Yolanda became a lifelong lover of learning.
And she still stands with

head high,

shoulders back,

spine straight.

Proud.

LOVE

FREEDOM

FAITH

TRIUMPH

Notes from the Authors

"The function of education is to teach one to think [critically].
Intelligence plus character—that is the goal of true education."
—Dr. Martin Luther King Jr.

As a young child, Yolanda Gladden believed Black people come from power and creativity, greatness and strength. Based on that belief, she made the wise decision to take the gift of a good education seriously and to become a lifelong reader and writer. She understood early on that in life, no one bothers a bare tree. Circumstances or even people can be unfair or unkind, but education is a ripe fruit ready to be enjoyed by each of us. It is a right owed to us all. In fact, life's lessons and schools are all around.

If home is where the heart is, school is where the mind thrives.

Much like homes, what a school looks like can vary, and the quality of the school, like the education one receives while attending, has little to do with where the school is physically located. The true measure of a school is how much and how often the minds nurtured within it grow, learn, expand, and evolve. And just like in a home, warmth, love, care, fairness, equality, togetherness, laughter, and safety in a school ensure a special space for all to feel wanted and welcome, just as everyone should.

—Dr. Pizzoli

Me on picture day.

I always loved hearing stories of how my mother and aunt protested injustice and unfair conditions alongside sixteen-year-old Barbara Johns in high school. They were the students who led a strike at Robert Russa Moton High School in Farmville, Prince Edward County, Virginia, on April 21, 1951. That protest—along with countless others—resulted in the landmark decision that they thought would change the country. It was their big breakthrough. And that's why the history of the *Brown v. Board of Education* case is well documented in books, movies, and museums.

School days.

But what most people don't know is that the decision makers in my hometown had their own plans: plans that would curtail progress, plans that would shut down public schools for five years, plans that are left out of mainstream history.

When this time period in Virginia history was finally documented, historians referred to us as the "Lost Generation" because we didn't attend formal public schools. Some families sent their kids out of the county, and many simply could not attend school. But I come from a proud, resourceful, and creative people. We weren't all lost, and we didn't accept injustice lying down. While activists did their part to fight the shutdown, we took our education and futures into our own hands. We threw out the concept of "schooling" and learned not only the basic curriculum but what it means to be Black and what it means to be responsibly intelligent.

Even though the schools were eventually desegregated, I'll never forget the real-life lessons taught to me by Mama, Aunt Dorothy, Uncle Tank, my church family, and my community.

I hope my story inspires everyone to stand up for what they believe in and to value education. I hope it sheds light on a hidden history and that it encourages us to still march forward toward change.

—Ms. Yolanda Gladden

The Road to Desegregation of the American School System

Many laws were passed, broken, and amended over the years before our nation fully desegregated American schools to give every child an equal education.

1849 The Massachusetts Supreme Court dismisses a case in which a father sues the city of Boston for denying his five-year-old daughter entry to a local all-white elementary school.

1868 The Fourteenth Amendment marks the right of all citizens to equal protection under the law.

1896 In the *Plessy v. Ferguson* case, the US Supreme Court deems racial segregation laws constitutional for public locations given that such places were of equal quality. This landmark ruling gives rise to the phrase "separate but equal."

1950 Thurgood Marshall, head of the NAACP Legal Defense and Education Fund, wins the *Sweatt v. Painter* and the *McLaurin v. Oklahoma State Regents for Higher Education* Supreme Court cases, challenging Jim Crow laws in higher education and setting important precedents for the *Brown v. Board of Education of Topeka* case.

1950 Gregory Swanson is the first Black student at a white school in Virginia when he enrolls in the University of Virginia School of Law.

1951 Students in Farmville, Virginia, protest unequal conditions and sue for an integrated school.

1951 Oliver Brown and the NAACP sue the Board of Education of Topeka, Kansas, for denying his daughter Linda Brown entry to the local white school.

1954 Thurgood Marshall and the NAACP represent the Browns as well as four other similar school segregation cases, including the Farmville, Virginia, lawsuit (*Davis v. County School Board*), consolidated under the *Brown v. Board of Education of Topeka* case, in the US Supreme Court. The Supreme Court delivers a ruling in which segregated schools are declared to be "inherently unequal," and orders the schools to be desegregated; *Plessy v. Ferguson* is overturned.

1954 Ethel Payne, a trailblazing Black journalist, asks President Eisenhower for his support in getting Congress to act on the *Brown v. Board of Education of Topeka* decision and begin the process of integrating schools. Her famous question draws attention to the fact that the US Supreme Court did not establish a specific time frame in their ruling. The president resists giving his support.

1955 The US Supreme Court rules that school districts must integrate "with all deliberate speed."

1956 US Senators Strom Thurmond from South Carolina and Harry Byrd from Virginia pen the "Southern Manifesto," a document in which they underline their disagreement with the US Supreme Court's *Brown v. Board of Education of Topeka* ruling and state their commitment to resist public school integration efforts.

1956 Virginia passes Massive Resistance laws to "prevent a single Negro child from entering any white school."

1957 Governor Orval Faubus mobilizes state troops in reaction to a federal court order to desegregate Little Rock, Arkansas's all-white high school. President Eisenhower reluctantly sends federal troops to end the violent mob and escort the Little Rock Nine, the first Black students of Little Rock Central High School, into the school. These actions become known as the Little Rock Crisis.

1958 Federal courts order nine white schools in Virginia to admit Black students, and Governor J. Lindsay Almond closes those schools in response.

1959 Virginia passes the Freedom of Choice plan, resulting in a few Black students applying to transfer to white schools, of which a small number are accepted.

1959–1963 Prince Edward County officials in Farmville, Virginia, close all public schools to avoid integrating them. White students attend private academies while Black students attend community-led schools in homes and churches. But a number of Black and white students do not receive a formal education at all during the shutdown of the public schools.

1960 Four Black six-year-old girls—Leona Tate, Tessie Prevost, Gail Etienne, and Ruby Bridges—desegregate two New Orleans, Louisiana, elementary schools. A white boycott and race riots break out, now known as the New Orleans School Desegregation Crisis.

1962 Riots break out at the University of Mississippi when James Meredith, a Black student, arrives on the Oxford campus to enroll.

1963 The Ford Foundation funds private schools for Black students. Prince Edward Free Schools open to provide free education to all children in the county.

1964 In a landmark ruling in the case of *Griffin v. School Board of Prince Edward County*, the US Supreme Court orders Prince Edward County in Virginia to reopen all public schools and to ensure integrated classrooms.

1964 The Civil Rights Act completely outlaws discrimination based on color, race, national origin, religion, or gender. It also declares racial segregation in schools, workplaces, and public spaces to be illegal.

1968 All public colleges in Virginia admit both white and Black students; the US Supreme Court ends "freedom of choice" plans.

1972– *Oklahoma City Public Schools v. Dowell* allows public schools to remain segregated in cases where desegregation orders have failed. In 1985, the Oklahoma City Board of Education overturns this decision and adopts a new plan to desegregate (the plan was controversial). By 1973, ninety percent of Black children in the South attend integrated schools. Yet, even today, we have a long way to go before schools are truly equal. According to "Modern Segregation," an Economic Policy Institute report by Richard Rothstein, by 2014, the typical Black student attends a school where only 29 percent of their fellow students are white. This is down from about 36 percent in 1980. And in 2016, a federal court orders the Cleveland School District in western Mississippi to desegregate its middle schools and high schools.

Forward Ever.

Sources and Further Reading

Note from the editor: Yolanda Gladden's oral history served as the main source of information for this book. Some stories were told to her from family and friends, and others are memories of her own firsthand experiences. This type of research is precious to the African diaspora. Oftentimes, our griots are our only means of preserving our history, and we thank them for all that they do to keep our legacy and truths alive.

"April 1951: Barbara Johns leads Prince Edward County Student Walkout." The Student Nonviolent Coordinating Committee (SNCC) Digital Gateway. www.snccdigital.org/events/barbara-johns-leads-prince-edward-county-student-walkout.

Green, Kristen. "Prince Edward County's Long Shadow of Segregation." The Atlantic, August 1, 2015. www.theatlantic.com/national/archive/2015/08/segregation-prince-edward-county/400256.

Heinemann, Ronald L. "Moton School Strike and Prince Edward County School Closings." Encyclopedia Virginia, January 21, 2014. www.encyclopediavirginia.org/moton_school_strike_and_prince_edward_county_school_closings.

June-Friesen, Katy. "Massive Resistance in a Small Town." Humanities, September/October 2013. www.neh.gov/humanities/2013/septemberoctober/feature/massive-resistance-in-small-town.

Kanefield, Teri. The Girl from the Tar Paper School: Barbara Rose Johns and the Advent of the Civil Rights Movement. New York: Harry N. Abrams, 2014.

Robert Russa Moton Museum, Farmville, Virginia. The former high school, now a National Historic Landmark and museum, is the birthplace of America's student-led civil rights revolution. www.motonmuseum.org.

Students entering entering the "free school," Mary E. Branch School, in Farmville, Virginia, in late 1963.